Small Change

Small Change

The Secret Life of Penny Burford

J. Belinda Yandell

CUMBERLAND HOUSE PUBLISHING
NASHVILLE, TENNESSEE

PUBLISHED BY
Cumberland House Publishing, Inc.
431 Harding Industrial Drive
Nashville, TN 37211
www.cumberlandhouse.com

Cover design: Unlikely Suburban Design
Text design: Lisa Taylor

Library of Congress Cataloging-in-Publication Data

Yandell, J. Belinda, 1963–
    Small change : the secret life of Penny Burford / J. Belinda Yandell.
        p. cm.
    ISBN 1-58182-304-5
    1. Housewives—Fiction. 2. Investments—Fiction. 3. Widowers—Fiction. I. Title.
    PS3625.A676 S6 2002
    813'.6—dc21

                                                        2002008801

Printed in the United States of America
1 2 3 4 5 6 7 8 — 07 06 05 04 03 02

THIS BOOK IS DEDICATED TO BOBBIE MCMILLAN YANDELL:
my Mother, my Friend, my Constant Reader
and the Inspiration for everything good and worthwhile
I've ever accomplished or ever hope to accomplish.

acknowledgements

No one but my friends and family will bother to read this, and I won't be offended at all if you skip this part. I feel a bit like some minor technician who's won an Academy Award, and so I'm going to cram in all the thanks I can.

Thanks to Jane Pepperdene, professor emeritus at Agnes Scott College for Women, who changed my life in more ways than she can ever know by bringing me to ASC.

To Bo Ball, also of ASC, the first great writer I was privileged to know. Read his book of beautiful short stories, *Appalachian Patterns*. Anything good and true that I know about the craft of writing, I learned from him.

To Suet Lim, my dear misplaced friend, whose example gave me the courage to try.

To Traci Cothron and Sam Wolverton at MediaBay Audio Books, for allowing me to get my foot in the door.

To my agent, Elizabeth Pomada, for saying yes when so many had said no.

To the entire staff of Cumberland House Publishing, particularly Ron Pitkin, Julie Jayne, and Lisa Taylor, my editor, for their faith, skill, and enthusiasm.

To Kelly Burch Cole, for being my Best Friend, unflagging cheerleader . . . and lending me her type-writer oh, so long ago.

To Carolyn Connelly Simons, for being the one friend who knows what it's like to sit in front of blank computer screen or typewriter wondering what in the heck happens next.

To my mother, Bobbie; my sister, Karen Yandell Pendergast; and my granny, Leona McMillan . . . because I love you all so very much and because the love you've given me all my life is the cornerstone of who and what I am.

And last, but certainly not least, my deepest gratitude to John Mitchell, without whom this book might not ever have seen print. Your friendship and support are appreciated more than I can express. Thank you, John, for having faith in me. . . .

Small Change

chapter one

It started with a single nickel in 1965. She didn't
know why she took it. Even in 1965, a nickel wasn't
worth as much as it used to be.

Usually she just swept up the coins and carried
them into the bedroom, where she dumped
them into the ashtray with a metallic plunk. But
that morning in the fall of 1965, she stood looking at the dirty silver disk lying on top of the
television cabinet for so long that it began to
look strange, the way a word repeated over and
over loses its normal rhythm. She stared at
Thomas Jefferson's profile and her mouth grew
moist with the memory of lemon drops and King
Leo peppermint sticks.

Maybe it was the memory of penny candy, the sweet bright colors of it. Or maybe it was remembering the excruciating choices required of a small girl with a single nickel clenched in a sweaty hand.

She could remember it so clearly, how she would stand slack-mouthed with concentration before the fat round jars on the counter of Friedman's Five and Dime, leaning her whole body against the counter that was nearly as tall as she was. She would point at her selections one by one—adding another smudgy fingerprint to the glass—occasionally pausing to count on her fingers and contemplate her options. Mr. Friedman, utterly patient, would hold the brown paper sack in the palm of one gigantic hand and grin at her sober deliberation.

Red and black licorice laces. Wide, white strips of multi-colored candy buttons that she peeled from the waxy paper with her front teeth. Taffy cylinders in waxy translucent wrappers that

Small Change

revealed just a hint of the pastels within, the fanned ends of the paper like butterfly wings. Rough crystalline wands of glittering rock candy. Root beer barrels, caramels, gumdrops that sparkled like solidified nuggets of a rainbow. Necco wafers that melted in sugary bliss upon her tongue. She had had so many choices back then.

She could remember not just the candy, but the store itself. Friedman's Five and Dime sat on Main Street between Halder's Feed and Hardware and the barber shop. Even from the sidewalk, Friedman's wide front windows captivated the imagination; behind the winking expanse of glass, each season brought a different landscape of longing. In summer, the display would include lawn chairs, shiny oscillating fans with teardrop blades, kites, roller skates, bicycles, and Fourth of July flags. In the fall, school supplies—book bags, pencil cases, stacks of Crayola boxes—would share the windows with rakes, Blue Willow dishes, and Halloween masks.

13

And Christmas! Oh, how the windows would shine with tinsel, wrapping paper, and toys: dolls, china tea sets, trucks, wagons, and stuffed animals of every shape, color, and size. Only the most expensive items—toys Penny would never own and hardly dared to dream of—went in the window; but she could imagine herself flying down the sidewalk on that Firestone Cruiser, its red fenders and headlight gleaming. The more common but still desirable jump ropes, jacks, and marbles were heaped in wire baskets along the shelves inside.

The air inside Friedman's was cool in the morning, but by late afternoon when the sun came slanting through the windows, the atmosphere became almost tangibly sticky, sugar dancing with the dust motes. Hardwood floors, blackened with age, creaked underfoot as the aroma of popcorn, peanuts, and caramel crept into the nostrils, vying for dominance with the sugar.

Small Change

The soda counter, a ribbon of shining chrome that ran down one side of the store, provided smells of its own: vanilla-, lemon-, cherry-, grape-, and strawberry-flavored delights. Around lunchtime, grease took precedence, from hamburgers and cheese sandwiches sizzling on the small, blackened grill.

Deeper into the store, other sundry scents eddied through that river of sun-warmed air: Wild Root hair tonic, Ivory soap, and talc. From the cosmetic counter came more cloying sweetness: big blue bottles of Evening in Paris and Blue Waltz perfume, dusting powders with unpronounceable French names, Westmore rouge and lipsticks, gardenia and lavender sachets in tiny satin bags.

She remembered Mr. Friedman's careless, rubbery smile and stubby crew-cut, the faint circles of perspiration in the armpits of his white shirt. His long sleeves were always rolled up to reveal forearms of thick, black hair. She had liked Mr. Friedman, though his hairy arms had once alarmed her. Sometimes she pushed eagerly into the store to find Mrs. Friedman behind the counter instead, and some of her anticipation would fade. Mrs. Friedman would fill the tiny bag with outward patience, but the corners of her lips tucked into her cheeks as if she was thinking of better things she might be doing. If the older girls happened to wander in and saunter, giggling, toward the cosmetics, Mrs. Friedman's eyes would narrow as she craned her neck to keep them in her sight.

Her mother shopped at the five-and-dime for the most tedious things: castor oil, thread, buttons, headache powders, yarn, and ribbon by the yard. Her mother would always examine the veils and the handkerchiefs, but she never bought them. Sometimes her mother paused to pick up a tube of lipstick in a garish shade of red or coral. She would examine it with a rueful and almost disapproving smile before returning it to the counter.

Small Change

"I could never wear that color," her mother sometimes remarked, bending low to her ear as if afraid someone might overhear. "Even if I wanted to."

Sometimes she accompanied her father, fresh from the barber shop on Saturday mornings, when he would purchase razors, a ball of twine, or shoe polish. Only on Saturdays with him would she be treated to an ice cream cone or shaved ice with strawberry syrup.

But mostly she went to Friedman's on her own, or with Molly Treener who lived next door, to buy candy, not just because she had a voracious sweet tooth, but because the penny-a-piece treats were all she could afford. That was back in the days when children could roam all over town in safety, when every adult knew where every child lived and to whom they belonged.

Even the name had been magical: penny candy. How old had she been before she realized they called it penny candy because of the price and not because it was meant for her—a small, skinny girl named Penny?

So on that morning of 1965, instead of carrying the coin into the bedroom, she had slipped that nickel into the pocket of her housedress. She kept right on dusting, blasting the cabinet with a hiss of Lemon Pledge. The singular weight of the coin slapped against her thigh for the rest of the day.

She could remember wondering if there was even such a thing as penny candy any more, and if there was, where did children buy it? By 1965, her candy-buying days were as long gone as Friedman's, and her own children had not yet been old enough for such things. Little Carl had been only three, and she didn't even let the pediatrician give him a sucker for fear he'd choke on it. Sandy was just a baby. But she remembered grieving that they might never know the joy of a single penny, or feel as rich as a Rockefeller with a whole nickel of their very own.

Small Change

"See a penny, pick it up," her daddy used to laugh, swooping her onto his shoulders. "And all day long you'll have good luck!"

He had called her his "lucky Penny." By 1999, the year she turned fifty-seven, her daddy was long dead, and no one cared about pennies anymore. People dropped them in store aisles and parking lots, and did not even bother to pick them up.

Mr. Friedman and his wife retired and moved to Florida in 1960, the year she married Roy. Every few years, a new sign or awning would appear over the front door, announcing a pet store, a beauty parlor, or a real estate office. In between these transformations, the storefront would sit empty and forlorn, causing Penny a pang of loneliness whenever she passed by.

She had been glad every time a new tenant moved into the old five-and-dime, usually slapping another coat of paint over the whitewashed brick exterior. The most recent sign was an

elegant wooden affair with gilded raised lettering: The Purple Peacock Tea Room.

The display windows that had once held all
the treasures of the universe now held a garden
of delicate greenery. The deep sill that once sup-
ported stacks of Blue Willow dishes and Radio
Flyers now held flower boxes of arching maiden-
hair fern, white cyclamen, and trailing English
ivy.

The paisley curtains—in a purple, green, and
yellow pattern Betty Colcamp had declared
unspeakably gaudy—were swagged to reveal white
tablecloths and vases of daisies, tulips, or sometimes irises. Waiters glided past in crisp white
shirts and black bow ties. Sandy had laughed
when Penny asked what kind of person went all
the way downtown just to have a cup of tea.

"It's a restaurant, Momma. They don't serve
just tea."

Sandy always seemed to be laughing at her
lately, not unkindly, but in the way she herself

had laughed when Sandy first started burbling questions only a mother could interpret. At least Sandy didn't roll her eyes the way her brother did. If Sandy was patronizingly kind, then Carl was impatient and vaguely embarrassed by his mother's ignorance.

"For Pete's sake, Ma," Carl had muttered. "Tea rooms are very 'in' right now."

In what? She had wanted to ask, but the twist of his lips had stilled her own.

That twist of his lips dismayed her most about her son. When he was born, she had been secretly relieved that Carl did not look like his father. Not that Roy was unattractive, far from it. But Roy's good looks were hard in a way Penny couldn't precisely define; he was a thickly built, massive man with features as mobile as graven stone. He had, in short, the looks of a man who could not—would not—be coddled, petted, and kissed, the way she yearned to coddle, pet, and kiss her baby boy, her firstborn.

Then, somewhere in puberty, Carl had betrayed her. He had started frowning in that tight, preoccupied way of his father's, an expression that hardened his still-soft features into an echo of Roy's.

Not that she didn't love Roy. He was a good provider, a fine father, and a hard worker who never called in sick, not even that time when she'd been sure he had walking pneumonia. He didn't drink; he didn't hit her; he didn't chase women. He kept the lawn and hedges neat as a pin and the gutters clean. He not only took out the garbage without being reminded, but he never failed to bring the cans back into the garage as soon as he came home from work on trash days. He was handy and conscientious around the house, oiling door hinges and fixing leaky faucets with a sober determination. It was just that . . . smirk. She didn't like to call it that, even to herself, but that's what it was. A smirk.

She didn't like that smirk any more than she

liked the way he emptied his pockets all over the house. She felt petty that it annoyed her so. Of all the marriages she knew, a sour expression and one bad habit weren't anything to complain about.

What bothered her most was that she couldn't remember ever seeing that particular expression before they were married. The smirk was like the defect she found in a marked-down blouse after she brought it home. She had been afraid to take the blouse back to the store; perhaps they would only tell her: "Of course, why do you think it was on the clearance rack?"

She didn't tell Roy about the blouse, either. He would only have smirked and said, "That's what you get for buying discount."

Then he would have wanted to know where she'd gotten the money for a blouse. He only gave her money for clothes twice a year: in the spring, to buy a new dress for Easter Sunday; and again in August, when he would hand her a birthday card—something only mildly sentimental, usually with flowers on the front—with two twenty-dollar bills inside. "Go and buy yourself something nice," he would say.

Perhaps he hadn't hidden the smirk while they were courting. Perhaps she just hadn't seen it any more than she had noticed the flaw in the seam of the blouse's sleeve. Her amazement at finding such a bargain had blinded her. Maybe it was only an expression he had grown into later, like the paunch above his belt buckle.

In the first years of their marriage, she had chided him affectionately about leaving the debris of his pockets all over the house. Gas receipts, bank stubs, half-empty packs of gum, buttons, keys, his pocketknife, and change formed a trail from the back door to their bedroom.

At first he had smiled and promised to do better. Over time the smile tightened and eventually slipped from his face. He began to nod, absently at first and then impatiently. At some point, he seemed to stop hearing her, and she grew to loathe the sound of her own nagging. The way he didn't hear her made her feel somehow less there.

For a time she gathered up the change, keys, and papers, putting each where she thought they belonged and feeling a small swell of pride at the way she'd restored the order of the world without saying a word. But Roy muttered as he stalked through the house, opening and closing drawers, fishing through pockets in the hamper, finally bellowing her name in exasperation.

She hadn't known where those things belonged after all. He accused her of losing phone numbers scribbled on matchbooks. She made him late for work because he couldn't find his keys, so cleverly hidden on the hook by the back door. She caused him to cut his hand on a rusty box cutter because his own knife wasn't in his pocket where it belonged.

Eventually, she had polished up an old brass ashtray that had been packed away. Silently she gathered up his miscellany, depositing it all into the shallow bowl on his dresser. He would never learn to empty his pockets directly into the ashtray, but this compromise seemed to work. She had a single place to put it all—one mess rather than half a dozen—and he had a place where he could easily reclaim his belongings at a glance. All she had to do was stop minding the untidiness of it.

The ashtray was nine inches in diameter with a wide, flat rim inscribed in circus-style lettering: A WOMAN IS ONLY A WOMAN, BUT A GOOD CIGAR IS A SMOKE. It was ugly and heavy, and its slogan struck her as faintly vulgar.

The ashtray had belonged to Roy's father, dead twelve years this Christmas of emphysema and Hav-A-Tampas. "Shiftless old coot," Roy would mutter whenever he looked at the ashtray.

She knew that shiftless was the worst thing a man could be, in Roy's mind. Yet he wouldn't let her throw the ashtray out, though neither she nor Roy smoked. She thought it might be the only thing his father had left him. The only *tangible* thing. Old Mr. Burford had left Roy plenty of other legacies, none of which could be hidden away as easily as an ugly ashtray.

The change soon began spilling over the ashtray's rim. Three silver dollars peeked out from under a scattering of copper and alloy, calling to her with a siren's song. Her father had given her a silver dollar once, on her twelfth birthday. She had spent it at Friedman's, not on candy that time but on a chocolate malt and a red yo-yo, the object of her longing for an entire summer.

When she offered to roll the coins, Roy had only shrugged behind his newspaper.

"Ain't worth the trouble."

"There must be at least twenty dollars in there. Maybe more—"

"No. Leave it be."

"But—"

"I ain't having Bill Colcamp's wife down at

the First American blabbing about how my wife has to roll pennies!"

"I just thought—"

"Lookit. Don't I take care of you? Don't I always put food on the table and clothes on your back and a roof over your head? Don't I?"

Beneath the annoyance of his words, she heard something else. A slightly desperate uncertainty that made her think of Plumrose canned ham, Christmas, and peeling white paint. She said no more about the coins, understanding that to do so would be to encroach too closely on Roy's private, posted territory.

chapter two

Penny Harper had grown up poor, though not as poor as Roy. Those nickels she had carried to Friedman's Five and Dime had been rare and treasured far above their worth, but as far as she knew, Roy had never run all the way to Friedman's with even a penny in his pocket. A silver dollar would have been beyond his greatest imaginings, as mythic as a unicorn or dragon.

She thought that being poor might be harder on a man, especially one as proud as Roy Burford. In grade school, he had skulked around the edges of the playground at recess, and always chose the back of the classroom except when the teacher forced them into alphabetical seating arrangements. She might never have noticed him at all, so assiduously did he work at making himself invisible.

But at lunchtime, Roy Burford could not escape her scrutiny or anyone else's. Because he could not afford the school lunch, he scraped cafeteria trays in return for a free hot meal. For reasons no one ever questioned—except possibly Roy, and Penny would never dare to ask him— he was not allowed to do this in the privacy of the kitchen, but instead performed his duty just inside the window where his classmates brought their finished trays.

Penny saw him at this chore every school day and wondered, at first, why he seemed so angry. He attacked each tray with a serving spoon, practically flinging the remains of mashed potatoes, lima beans, and turnip greens into the plastic-lined trash barrels. Later, as she came to understand the subtle cruelties of the schoolyard, she would wonder why his mother didn't send him to school with a homemade lunch to spare him this shaming. Lots of the farm kids—generally the poorest of the poor—brought lunch pails or sacks filled with cold biscuits, the molasses making greasy stains on the well-worn brown paper.

He never looked anybody in the eye, only stood with his head angled so that all she saw was the line of his mouth and his flaring nostrils. He hardly spoke to anybody, but everybody knew his daddy drank and couldn't hold a job. In the shorthand of a small town, where everyone was pigeonholed practically from birth, Roy was simply "that drunk Burford's youngest boy."

Penny, likewise, had been "the preacher's daughter." As pastor of Grace Baptist, her daddy had shone like an apostle in her eyes. Brother Harper was a tall, slender man who always wore a long-sleeved shirt and tie, even in the heat of high Georgia summer. His thick, dark hair began to gray when Penny was still very young, giving him a dignity at odds with the gentle good-humor in his crinkling eyes.

When she was growing up, Penny had loved Christmastime the best, not because of Santa Claus, the decorations, or even because it was the baby Jesus' birthday. She loved Christmas because that was when she was allowed to help her daddy nearly every night. In his little office at the church, they would sort the cans of donated food, cleaning off dust and gluing down peeling labels. She would help him arrange the foodstuffs in boxes, planning nutritious meals in her head for imagined families. A bag of beans for this one; a can of green peas for that one; and, oh, here was a can of sweet potatoes, just the thing for a Christmas dinner! So many choices to make, trying so hard to be fair, to make sure every box got a variety. If she gave one box a jar of beets—and she loathed beets so much herself that she couldn't imagine anyone might like them—she would try to make up for it with something extra, perhaps a can of Vienna sausages or a surprising tin of Baker's chocolate.

Her mother and the other church ladies would be busy mending, washing, and ironing the donated clothing. The stocking of the boxes and the wrapping of small, second-hand toys were chores she alone shared with her daddy. They would deliver them together, just the two of them, while her mother labored in the kitchen over Christmas dinner and waited for their return.

As they drove around town making their rounds, her daddy would always talk about Jesus in that strangely soft yet sonorous voice of his.

But it wasn't Jesus that Penny thought about as she handed out the presents to the smallest children on their list. When they clamored and clapped, their eyes shining, she thought of Santa Claus. She understood why the jolly fat man spent his life giving toys to strangers. By the time they returned home, Penny's cheeks were rosy as much from a boundless joy as the winter's chill.

All that had ended the day she followed her daddy up the front steps of a ramshackle white house and the door was opened, not by a stranger, but by someone she knew.

Ten-year-old Roy Burford's face was a moist, hot red as he peered around his mother and saw Penny standing there, holding a canned ham. His amber eyes, whose color she had never noticed before, locked on hers with a ferocity that nearly knocked the wind right out of her lungs.

Roy's mother, she thought, couldn't be much older than her own, but this woman in a faded, unraveling brown cardigan and floral-print skirt—incongruously light in both weight and color for December—reminded Penny more of her Grandmother Harper, who was nearly sixty. Mrs. Burford had a sagging, colorless face under a frizz of hair the exact hue of dead oak leaves. She wore thick wool socks and a pair of men's vinyl bedroom slippers on her feet. She looked like a washrag that had been used hard, then wrung out by vicious, twisting fists and left to dry in an unsmoothed lump.

Mrs. Burford stood there a long moment, one hand clutching the wooden frame of a rusting screen door as if she feared Brother Harper might try to push his way into the house. Then her flat, lint-colored eyes moved to the box tucked under his left arm, to the grocery sack full of tissue-wrapped parcels balanced in the crook of his other arm, finally settling on the canned ham clutched to Penny's chest. The woman seemed to shake herself to full consciousness as if the effort was something she could scarcely afford and resented the necessity of. When she stretched her lips, her smile held even less warmth than the interior of the house into which she half-heartedly ushered them.

Inside the house, there was no hint of the season. Poverty was not an adequate excuse, for

Penny had seen other more desperate shacks still make some kind of effort. If there was not a scraggly cedar tree draped with paper chains and tinfoil stars, there was at least a red ribbon on the door, crudely embellished woolen socks hung by the fireplace or pine branches laid over the mantel. Just this morning, the three little Pearson girls had shown her the Nativity scene they'd recreated from construction paper, cardboard boxes, and Popsicle sticks; they proudly pointed out the Baby Jesus, a scrap of cloth and a wooden bead resting in a matchbox. Penny, in gratitude, had given them the peppermint stick in her coat pocket, the one Mr. Benning at the barber shop had given her the day before.

But here, in the Burford house, there was nothing that even hinted at Christmas. The front room was dim with thin, drawn curtains and curling wallpaper of brown cabbage roses. Penny stared at her feet, trying not to notice the threadbare brown carpet and the pervasive odor of souring turnips and kerosene. When she glanced at the fireplace, she saw that it did not burn wood, but newspaper and assorted trash. The label of an oatmeal box crisped and curled into a blackened fist before her eyes.

Two little boys—perhaps five and six years old—broke off wrestling on the floor and leapt to their feet, eyeing the bag and box in her daddy's arms with wary interest. A girl, perhaps a year older or younger than Penny, stood in the doorway of the kitchen. She balanced a pasty-faced infant on her bony hip, her attitude one of practiced carelessness that contrasted oddly with her youth. She stared at Penny and wiped her flannel sleeve under her nose.

Mrs. Burford accepted the box with a murmur so faint Penny could not determine exactly what she said. Or perhaps she spoke quite clearly and only the roaring of blood through Penny's ears prevented her from hearing.

"Penny, honey?" her daddy whispered gently,

bending slightly to offer the grocery bag. "You wanna pass out the presents?"

Roy's younger brothers, understanding finally what was in the bag, shuffled toward her. One of them mumbled "thank you," then fell to the floor and ripped into the paper.

"Awright!" he breathed, holding up a plastic bag filled with green army men. His brother merely grunted at the jacks and red rubber ball, then snatched up one of the army men and made machine-gun sounds.

When the girl came forward, Penny held out a parcel. The girl only stared.

"That sure is a pretty ribbon you got in your hair," she said tonelessly.

"Um, thank you," Penny murmured. When the girl still made no move to take the present, Penny's free hand moved to the back of her head, to the enormous velvet bow her mother had fixed there that morning. Her eyes stung as she tugged it free.

Small Change

"You can have it. Merry Christmas."

The girl smiled, just a little, as she took the ribbon. For a moment, Penny felt that flicker of joy fighting to rekindle in her chest.

Then she saw Roy, leaning his elbows on the back of the sofa, his brow heavy. She laid the other presents on the sofa cushion, struggling to remember what she had chosen for this family based only the ages and sexes of its members. A blanket for the baby, a blouse for the mother, and a socket set for the unseen father—and a tiny toy truck for Roy.

She followed her daddy out the front door, and had just stepped onto the porch when she heard a shrill, feminine shriek from the living room. Suddenly Roy burst through the door. He threw something red into her startled face, then retreated quickly into the house and slammed the door.

Penny looked down at her feet where the velvet ribbon seemed to bleed, too red, on the peeling boards. When she made no move towards it, her daddy moved back to where she stood, frozen, and took her by the elbow.

She held her shame and disappointment in tight fists on the long walk back down the porch steps, across the yard that was more dirt than grass. As she stood waiting for her daddy to open the car door, she looked back towards the house. The blaze of red on the porch drew her eye like an accusation.

She scrambled inside the car, sliding across the tuck-and-roll upholstery of the old Ford. Her breath caught painfully in her throat as something deep inside her tightened. Tears rushed into her eyes.

"I—I d-d-on't un-derstand," she hiccuped. "I w-w-was just trying to d-do something nice. Why did h-he do that, Daddy? Why?"

"I don't know, honey." Her daddy shook his head, reaching out to pat her shoulder. "Some people are awful proud. It's hard for them to accept charity."

"B-b-but charity is a good thing, idn't it?" she wailed. Even halfway down the road, with the white house out of sight, her stomach still trembled violently. "The Bible says the g-greatest of these is charity, don't it?"

"It's hard to explain, Penny." Her daddy sighed. "It embarrasses some people. The Burfords don't go to church too often, so they don't know you and me very well. Maybe that little boy was like some people who think it reflects badly on them to accept something he didn't work for."

"But I give that ribbon to his sister, not to him! I wanted to, 'cause she liked it! It was just plain mean and hateful for him to take it away from her like that and then just throw it at me—"

"No, it wasn't a nice thing for him to do. But whatever he did, it doesn't change the fact that you acted with love in your heart. God knows that, and so do I. Maybe Roy will figure it out in time, too."

"But people take toys from S-Santa Claus! They don't feel bad t-taking stuff from him."

"Ah," her daddy sighed. "Santa Claus is—different."

"But why?" Penny scooted onto her knees, leaning against her daddy's shoulder, desperate for comfort. "He's a stranger, mostly. And he gives kids stuff that they don't even need, just 'cause they ask for it."

"Well, I suppose that makes a difference to some people. Santa Claus gives things to everybody, not just to poor people. You see, Penny, that little boy back there was embarrassed because he knows you, and you know him. He feels bad 'cause you know that his own parents haven't got money for food and presents."

"But that ain't his fault," Penny insisted.

Her daddy's mouth got tight. For a long moment he didn't speak. Finally he cleared his throat.

Small Change

"Penny, you know what gossip is?"

"Yes, sir." Penny sat back down in the seat. "Gossip is saying bad things about other people behind their back."

"That's right. Now, tell me truthfully. You ever heard people in this town talking about Roy or his family?"

"Well—" Penny hesitated. Was listening to gossip as much a sin as repeating it? "Yes, sir. I guess so."

"Well, if you've heard it, I reckon Roy's heard it, too. I'm sure Roy loves his momma and daddy, just as much as you love me and your momma. Now, how would you feel if you heard somebody repeating bad things about me?"

"I guess I'd feel pretty bad. Then I'd have to pray for Jesus to forgive me after I walloped 'em."

As soon as the words passed her lips, she wished she could take them back. But her daddy surprised her by tipping back his head and laughing until she thought she saw tears in his eyes.

She had never gone with him again. If her father was disappointed, he never pressed her. She still helped him collect the canned goods, sort and repair the donated toys, even wrap the gifts with exquisite care, but she would not go with him. That her joy might be gained at the cost of another's pain was something Penny could not bear.

chapter three

She tiptoed around Roy Burford after that disastrous Christmas, not quite ignoring him but taking care never to look directly at him. Yet she was always aware of his stiff, straight back and carefully blank expression, the ill-fitting clothes that looked as if Roy had tried ironing them himself.

It was only four years later, when they both entered high school, that Penny felt it safe to smile at Roy when she passed him the halls.

Even as a freshman, Roy already towered over the other boys in their class. His shoulders were wider, his neck as thick as a pine stump. It would be years after they were married before Penny learned the whole story of how Luther Skinner, the Tigers' coach, came to Roy and practically begged him to come to the tryouts. When Roy explained that he had to work after school and didn't have time to chase after a football, Coach Skinner had found Roy a job at the high school. His duties were light, mostly cleaning the athletic equipment and polishing the basketball court in the gym.

"I'll give you the keys to the place," Coach Skinner said. "You kin do the job at night, after practice, when everybody's gone home."

Roy was never quite popular; his pride was too prickly and his grim determination kept his peers at arm's length. But his place on the team seemed to lighten the chip he carried on his broad shoulders through the halls of Cairo High School. It didn't hurt that the Tigers won the State Championship in both his junior and senior year, and got to the Regional Championship when he was a freshman and sophomore. Football gave Roy a chance to carve some other identity for himself than "that drunk Burford's boy."

George Whitfield, the senior quarterback, sat in front of Penny in geometry. One day, when he turned to ask if he could borrow a pencil, she found the courage to ask him something that had been puzzling her for weeks.

"Why do they call Roy Burford 'the Rock?'"

"Hell, Coach Skinner started calling him that," George had grinned, showing the large white teeth that, along with his mop of blonde hair, were his most attractive feature. "'Cause when it comes to blocking out on the field, Roy is one sumbitch that will not be moved!"

Penny's girlfriends—and all the other girls in the school, for that matter—would casually eye the table where the football players sat in the cafeteria.

"Well, I think he's kinda cute," Sarah Butters sighed. "But he's so big! I'd be scared to get into the backseat with that one—"

"I wonder if he's that big all over," Hilda Green whispered, raising her penciled eyebrows over a sly grin, setting the other girls into gales of shrieking giggles.

Penny merely sipped at her milk, uncertain she understood the innuendo but not liking the sound of it. No one had ever even held her hand yet, let alone invited her into the backseat. She figured being the preacher's daughter had something to do with it.

"Well, Stevie Hicks told me he's a real straight arrow," Barbara Miller said. "He don't even drink."

When Hilda and Sarah didn't look as if they believed her, Barbara pushed on.

"No, seriously! Stevie said that after the game with Thomasville last week, they got Billy's older brother to buy 'em some beer and a bottle of whiskey. Then a bunch of 'em went and parked all their cars out in Mr. Parker's pasture, you know how they do—"

Small Change

"No, we don't know, Barb," Hilda smiled, cutting her eyes at Sarah. "But it sounds like you might been out in that pasture a time or two yourself—"

This brought more shrill laughter, though Barbara glared.

"You wanna hear this or not? Stevie said they was all getting pretty plastered when they realized Roy wadn't there anymore."

"Where'd he go?" Sarah asked. "He don't have a car. What'd he do? Walk home from Parker's?"

Barbara shrugged.

"Stevie didn't know. He said Roy was always doing that, just wandering off without a word whenever somebody brings out a bottle. Stevie figures it's 'cause of his daddy. You know ol' man Burford ain't been sober in a coon's age."

As Penny looked at Barbara's round cheeks and cherry red lips, at Hilda's penciled eyebrows and at Sarah's chipped magenta fingernails, the knowledge hit her quite suddenly: I don't really like these girls. They've been my friends since third grade, but I don't really like them at all.

Over the next few weeks, Penny sought out other company at lunchtime. She knew Betty Boone and Louise Jenkins from church, and they accepted her at their table eagerly. Betty had already been dating Billy Colcamp since ninth grade. Since Billy and Roy were friends—both on the football team, though Billy seldom got to play—it was Betty who suggested a double date.

"Roy's quiet," Betty said. "But he's real nice. It's just that he doesn't have a car, so he hates to ask girls out."

They went to the drive-in with Betty and Bill in the front seat. Penny and Roy sat stiffly in the back, as far apart as two people in the same automobile could be. When Betty and Bill began snuggling, Roy asked Penny if she'd like to walk to the concession stand with him.

"That'd be nice," Penny had breathed gratefully. He bought her a cherry Coke and, instead of walking back to the car, suggested they sit at one of the picnic tables.

"Movie's pretty bad, anyway," he said softly. "Unless, you wanted to watch it—"

"Oh, no," Penny said quickly. "You're right. It's not very good. I don't like scary movies very much."

She couldn't even remember the name of the movie, only that it was something silly about a mummy.

"Me, either," Roy said.

He had not bought a soda for himself, Penny noted with some concern. When she offered the cup to him, he shook his head and said he wasn't thirsty.

"Besides, that stuff's not good for you. All that sugar makes my teeth hurt."

"What kind of movies do you like?" Penny asked.

"Um . . . I like westerns. They're usually pretty good."

"You like Elvis?"

"Sure. Don't everybody?"

"My daddy says he cain't stand Elvis," Penny giggled, leaning forward as if confessing a secret. "I think he only says that 'cause my momma thinks he's cute."

chapter four

Roy had grown into a big man—six foot, four inches in his stocking feet, two hundred and fifty-four pounds, with a thick, tubular neck and hulking shoulders. The day after graduation, he got a job at the freight yard. Now Roy was a foreman, bringing home nearly thirty-five thousand a year before taxes. They had steak every Saturday and pot roast every Sunday. Roy watched his twenty-seven-inch satellite television from his enormous leather Lazy Boy in the den of the three-bedroom, one-and-a-half bath, aluminum-sided house.

Every three years Roy traded in the pickup and Caddy for newer models, even when Penny tried to tell him she didn't need a new car. It was a ritual she dreaded, standing in the dealership and pretending to study the tire charts as Roy commenced what he called "jewin' em down."

Once the deal was done, Roy always drove down Main Street so slowly that cars behind them honked. He cruised by Bill Colcamp's house, stopping when Bill cut off the lawn mower and ambled to the curb.

Roy never bought a car on a rainy Saturday.

The two men would grin as they surveyed the Caddy, talking of engines, carburetors, and mileage. At some point, Roy would jerk his thumb toward the sticker on the window.

"Can you believe what they wanted? You just gotta know how to handle them fellas."

"You got a good deal?"

"Sweet as a sixteen-year-old cherry," Roy would whisper with a grin.

And she always pretended not to hear.

She had borne him two healthy children who

had never scraped trays in the cafeteria, who began school every year in clothes so new they complained of the scratchiness. Carl had played football and basketball; Sandy had been a cheer-leader and student body president. Both Sandy and Carl had gone to college. When both the children moved away, it was a certain sign that their parents had succeeded. The only children who stayed in the old hometown were shiftless: managers at fast food restaurants, in trouble with the law or pregnant before graduation.

It should have been enough for Roy. But sometimes she still saw his nostrils flare, saw him angle his face away from her. Roy had an anger inside him and not even a new Caddy every three years or the thickest cut of sirloin could put it out. She saw it the first time she brought home the wrong brand of coffee because it had been on sale. She saw it whenever he dug his wallet from his back pocket and opened it with thick, plundering fingers.

He always carried a wad of greenbacks with a hundred-dollar bill on the outside. That hundred embarrassed her, made her heart cringe for him even as she hated the sight of it. Whenever she saw that hundred, she was standing on his front porch all over again, clutching a canned ham to her chest with both hands. He'd no more break that hundred than tip the waitress at Ponderosa more than ten percent. In more than twenty years of marriage, she had never seen him spend that hundred-dollar bill. She wondered if it had been the same bill all along or if he changed it periodically at the bank for a crisp new one.

It was strange to her that he cast the coins aside with so little care. He would never bother with exact change; instead he plunked down a twenty or a ten and watched hawk-eyed (but pretending not to) while the clerk counted the change back into his big, callused hand. Once he was sure he'd gotten exactly what was owed, he dismissed the coins until he got home. Only then would he dig out the accumulation of metal and scatter it over the kitchen counter, the top of the television, or the coffee table. Sometimes she even found a pile of coins on the back of the commode in the bathroom.

Maybe it was because the jingle in his pockets annoyed him or because the weight broke the neat pleats he'd taught her to iron into his pants. He liked them just so. When they first married, it had taken her two weeks of secret practice— ironing the same pair of pants, over and over, concentrating so hard that she got a headache— trying to get it right.

Roy paid the bills himself. She wasn't even sure exactly where he kept the checkbook. He frequently called the phone company or the electric service to question the validity of the charges. The new 911 fee on the phone bill infuriated him.

"What the hell do I pay taxes for? Why do I have to pay just to make sure the fire trucks can find my house? Bastards'll nickel and dime me to death."

Every Monday he counted out the house money: ninety dollars for groceries in ten-dollar bills. When the kids were at home, the grocery allotment had been higher, and sometimes he'd even forgotten to check the receipts. When it was just the two of them again, she was back to justifying every cent.

"You paid $2.49 a pound for bacon? Jeez, Penny. Didn't I tell you never to pay more than $1.99 for bacon?"

When she explained that the cheaper brand of bacon had been the same one he'd deemed all fat and grease at yesterday's breakfast, he smirked and said no more about it. It hardly mattered. If it wasn't the price of bacon, it was something else.

"I know you had a coupon for that. . . . Did you forget the coupons again? Hell, Pen, can't you remember anything? You think I'm made of money?"

Small Change

He never gave her money for gas. She had an Exxon card for that. When the bill came, he sometimes tapped a particular item with his fingernail.

"The fourteenth. Fourteen dollars and thirty-four cents. The price of gas ain't gone up that much. It don't take more than nine or ten to fill up the Caddy."

"I had them check the oil. He said it was a half-a-quart low."

"And you believed him? Jeez, don't ever buy oil at the gas station. Those guys just sit and wait for women like you. I've told you a dozen times. *Western Auto*."

"But Western Auto doesn't take the gas card."

He had stared at her a moment, squinting as if trying to determine whether she was mouthing off or just offering information.

"Next time some guy says you need oil, you tell me. I'll tell you whether you need oil or not."

chapter five

She was sure she'd intended to put that first nickel into the ashtray with the other coins, but for some reason, she had carried it around in her pocket all day. Every time she felt the weight of it against her thigh, she had thought to herself: I could just keep it. It's only a nickel. Roy doesn't even want it, so it's not as if I'm stealing anything.

That night, she had put the nickel in the bottom drawer of her jewelry box.

Two days later, Roy left another smattering of coins on the kitchen counter. She slipped another nickel and a dime into her pocket, and put the rest in the ashtray.

A day later, Roy left six quarters, two dimes and four pennies on the coffee table in the den. She didn't put any of it in the ashtray.

She put her stolen coins into a plastic change purse, a ten-year-old souvenir from Panama City. Roy might sometimes look in her wallet but he never touched the change purse.

She considered taking only the pennies or the quarters, but Roy might notice that. Instead she took a coin in each denomination from whatever he left lying around.

As the change purse grew heavier, she began to fret that its very bulk would attract his attention. So she hid the change purse in the bottom of a box of Tampax in the bathroom closet. Roy would never touch that box, let alone look inside of it.

She had never kept a secret from him. At first, the guilt permeated every moment in his presence. Every time he cleared his throat, she expected a declaration that he knew what she was up to. But it never came, and he never noticed that the coins in the ashtray remained constant.

Six months later, Penny lifted the heavy change purse from the Tampax box and the seams of the old vinyl split. Silver and copper poured onto the tiled floor of the bathroom with the clatter of metallic rain.

On her hands and knees, she scooped handfuls of coins back into the Tampax box and carried it into the kitchen. On the Formica tabletop, she arranged stacks of pennies, nickels, dimes, and quarters.

Twenty-seven dollars and eighty-four cents.

She sighed with pleasure. She had a whole two dollars more than the price of that beautiful purple dress in the window of Gaffer's Department Store. She could drive right down there, plunk her money on the counter and buy that dress. She had always wanted something just that color.

Then her heart sank. How would she explain it to Roy? Something dull might slip past him, but not that purple dress. She couldn't spend the money, and she couldn't give it back to Roy. Not after all this time. She had no choice but to keep hiding it. And yet she couldn't stop herself from adding to it, just a coin or two at a time.

For some reason, just knowing the money was there soothed her. Now, when Roy griped about the rising price of gas or an increase in property taxes, Penny didn't get that same twisted feeling in her stomach. She would think about the hidden money and figure things couldn't be all that bad if Roy still left so much money lying all around the house. When he agonized over the rainy day he just knew would one day come, Penny visualized an umbrella made of quarters, dimes and nickels.

By the time Sandy started school in 1970, Penny's secret money was hidden all over the house. Neat rolls of quarters and dimes were still

Small Change

hidden in the Tampax box in the bathroom closet, but her old cosmetic case, in the top of her closet, was also full of dull red rolls of pennies. Inside her old rubber boots, the ones she never wore anymore, were more nickels. Rolls of all denominations were hidden in a big tin that had once held a Christmas fruitcake, pushed way back on a high shelf in the pantry.

The fruitcake tin had nearly been the end of it.

She had come home from Monday night's Bible Circle to find *Gunsmoke* blaring and the Lazy Boy empty. She walked into the kitchen and there was Roy, staring into the open pantry with a frown of deep concentration etched into his features.

"What are you doing?"

"What does it look like? I'm looking for somethin' to eat."

"But I left you a plate of pot roast in the fridge—"

"Well, I'm still hungry. That little bit, you

shoulda just fed it to the dog. Don't we have any Vienna sausages? Or crackers? Jeez, the money you spend on food, and there's not a damn thing in this house to eat."

"I'll fix you something, if you'll just go sit down—"

"What's this? Fruitcake?"

"But you hate fruitcake!" A fist of panic around her heart made her voice squeak.

"No, I hate your momma's fruitcake." His hand reached high for it, but his fingers couldn't quite grasp the shiny, smooth rim. "This here says it comes from Claxton. We get this last Christmas? Or the Christmas before?"

"There's nothing in it!"

She squeezed between him and the pantry door, putting her hands on his chest as if she would push him back.

For a split second, his eyes stared down at her. His lips went tight, pressing into a narrow line the color of raw liver. She could hear him thinking: What the hell is the matter with you?

"I mean—" she stammered, pulling the corners of her mouth into what she hoped was a soothing, maternal expression. "I just use the tin for storing meal. That's all. There's no fruitcake, honey. That tin must be eight or nine years old. Go watch your program and I'll make you a Spam sandwich."

The next day, with both the kids at school and Roy at work, she emptied every hiding place. She loaded all of the rolls into an old book bag of Carl's and staggered as she carried it out to the car.

She didn't dare go to First American where they knew her. Betty Colcamp was head teller now, and she might mention something to Bill, who would surely tell Roy. Instead she drove twenty-eight miles to the Farmer's Union in Valdosta.

When she arrived back home two hours later, Penny sat in the driveway for a long time, unable to stop staring at the register of the stiff new passbook. $634.43, it read. The teller had had to write the number in because Penny's hands were shaking too much to hold the pen.

Now the Tampax box held nothing but a handful of loose change and the passbook.

Once a month, she drove to Valdosta and made a deposit. The clerk sometimes sighed as she pushed the rolls across the counter, but Penny had grown accustomed to it. Money was money, wasn't it?

Then one day the teller looked at her deposit slip and excused herself. Penny felt her heart thump queerly, certain that the woman would return and say, "We've called your husband, Mrs. Burford."

But instead a smiling young man rose from his desk and accompanied the teller back to the window. He extended his hand to Penny and asked if she would come over to his desk.

"Is something wrong?"

"Oh, no," he assured her. "It's just that I

wanted to talk to you about a better use of your capital—"

"My what?"

"Your money, Mrs. Burford. You've been a loyal customer of our bank for five years now, and we couldn't help noticing that you never take money out." He chuckled hollowly. "I wish my wife were half as interested as you seem to be in saving money rather than spending it."

The rest of his words were confusing and mostly incomprehensible. Something about interest, mutual funds, and certificates of deposit.

"I don't understand," Penny said. "You mean I can't just keep the money in a checking account?"

"Of course, you can, Mrs. Burford. That's absolutely fine. But wouldn't you like to put your money to work for you? Right now it's just sitting here, doing nothing."

He explained it all again, as patiently as a schoolteacher.

"You mean the bank will pay me just for keep-

ing my money in a special kind of account?" She
was aghast.

He nodded.

"Money's not really that important, in and of
itself, is it?" he smiled. "It's what you do with it
that counts."

It's what you do with it that counts. That phrase
kept echoing in her head all the way home. It
sounded a lot like something her daddy used
to say.

"Having faith is wonderful," he often said,
both from his pulpit and from the head of the
dinner table, "but it's what you do with it that
matters."

She pulled the Caddy into the parking lot
without even thinking about it. She had seen
their commercials, of course, and passed the
brightly-lit building every time she went to the
Piggly Wiggly, but she had never been inside the
Burger King. Roy said fast food wasn't that fast
and it sure wasn't food. Ponderosa was the only

restaurant Roy would patronize; he always approached the food bar like a man aiming to settle a score. Getting his money's worth, he called it, even though he scoffed at the wastefulness of nearby diners who left food on their plates.

Penny didn't like steak, though she didn't dare tell Roy that. Nor did she like Ponderosa much. She could never forget the time Roy had reduced Sandy to tears by insisting that if she put it on her plate, she had to eat it, every last mouthful.

She felt naked as she stepped inside the restaurant. It was bright and clean, full of hard-edged plastic colors. Behind the counter, a teenage girl with a bored expression cracked gum.

"Can I take your order?"

Penny stared at the back-lit menu boards. She had no idea what to order. Every full-color picture jumped at her.

"What do you recommend?"

The teenager blinked and swiveled her pale

blue eyes toward the ceiling, then back at Penny.

"Huh?"

"I'm sorry." Penny offered her most polite smile. "I've never eaten here before."

"You're kidding, right?"

She almost turned and ran. Then she remembered the passbook in her purse and straightened her spine. She had a new beaded change purse full of quarters, dimes, and nickels, not enough to roll yet. She might as well do something with that money instead putting it back in the tampon box.

It's what you do with it that counts.

"I'd like your biggest and best hamburger. Which one would that be?"

The girl grinned slyly and slid her eyes over to a boy occupied with dumping fries into hot grease.

"A Whopper, I guess." The girl shrugged. "Or a double Whopper."

"All right. I'd like a double Whopper."

"What do ya want on it?"

Small Change

"Whatever comes on it will be fine, thank you."

"Everything? You want fries?"

"French fries?"

The girl blinked again. This time she brought her hand up to her mouth.

"Uh-huh."

"That would be very nice."

"Large?"

"Um . . . yes."

"Anything to drink?"

She squinted at the menu again. So many choices . . . Roy didn't like soda pop. He claimed it rotted your teeth and that the carbonation ate into your stomach lining. At home they drank iced tea.

"Um . . . a Sprite, please." She had never had a Sprite, but she liked the cool green bottles on the shelves at the Piggly Wiggly.

"Small, medium, or large?"

"Medium, please."

Penny was giddy with relief as she carried the tray to a small table near the window. A young mother was dividing French fries between two small girls.

"She's got more than me," one of them whined.

"No, she doesn't. You watched me count them out. You both have exactly the same number of fries."

Penny looked around to find out if she was supposed to leave the food on the tray while she ate. The young mother had discarded her tray on an empty table. Across the room, a middle-aged man hunched over his meal, tray still in place. She supposed it was optional.

She wondered what Roy would say if he could see her here, unwrapping the big sandwich from its paper, licking off the ketchup that smeared her hand.

It was the best hamburger she'd ever tasted.

She sipped her Sprite, liking the way it

seemed to sparkle on her tongue with the sugary bliss of penny candy.

Maybe next time she'd order a milkshake. Strawberry.

chapter six

She stopped at the Burger King every Wednesday before going to the Piggly Wiggly. In a couple of months, she had sampled everything on their menu, including the little apple pies.

Later on, she was ready to try something different. After all, there were lots of restaurants around town that she had never set foot in, and she had plenty of money in her purse. She figured she could eat lunch just about anywhere in town on thirty-seven dollars and eighty-two cents.

This time, she headed downtown. She drove around and around the square until she found a parking space big enough for the Caddy.

She got out of the car and stood on the sidewalk, smoothing the wrinkles from her best skirt.
Taking a deep breath, she walked toward the
door of the Purple Peacock Tea Room.

A smiling young man in a crisp white shirt
and black bow tie looked up from behind the little wooden desk.

"Good morning, madam."

Penny looked around uncertainly at all the
empty tables, then glanced at her watch. It was
only eleven fifteen.

"Are you open? I can come back later—"

"No, no," he insisted. "Would you like a table?
Will anyone be joining you?"

She shook her head.

The purple carpet under her feet was so thick
that she felt like Neil Armstrong bouncing across
the moon as she followed him to a small table
draped in white linen.

He pulled out a chair of delicate white wicker.
Its bottom was covered by a cushion upholstered

in the same purple, green and yellow paisley as the curtains in the windows. She sat down stiffly, her spine inches from the back of the chair.

"Would you care to see our wine list?" Without waiting for her to answer, he offered her a leather binder with a gold tassel. She took it because she didn't know what else to do.

He began rattling off a list of the day's specials. She wasn't sure he was speaking English until she caught the words *mushrooms* and *chicken*.

"I . . . I've never eaten here before," she confessed in a soft voice.

"The Veal Marsala is very good, as are the beef medallions sautéed with sherry—"

"I'll have— I'll have that chicken thing you mentioned. You did say it was chicken, didn't you?"

His smile waned slightly before fixing again on his lips.

"Very good, madam. And to drink?"

"Do you have Sprite?"

"Um, no ma'am. I'm afraid not. We have an extensive wine list, along with tea, mineral water, and coffee. With the chicken, I'd recommend a glass of our house Chablis."

She didn't know what Chablis was, but she liked the sound of the word. Chablis. It sounded every bit as elegant as the white napkin on the plate in front of her, cleverly folded into the shape of a bird.

The chicken was wonderful, cooked in some kind of thick, creamy gravy so delicious that Penny wished she had some biscuits to sop it up with. But all the waiter brought was a basket of hard, dry bread. It surprised her that such a nice restaurant served stale rolls.

The Chablis turned out to be wine. She wrinkled her nose at it first, touching her tongue to it suspiciously and finding it wasn't even cold. But she drank it anyway. It got better with every sip. By the time the girl came around with a tray full of desserts, Penny felt all warm and rosy on the inside.

She pointed eagerly at a glass of chocolate pudding, but blanched when the girl told her it was mousse.

"Moose?" she repeated. "You serve that as a dessert?"

"Yes-s-s-s." The girl drew the word into a long hiss of uncertainty as she blinked down at Penny. She had a sweet, wide face that looked as if it belonged in high school, not in a restaurant in the middle of a school day. "It's very good. I promise."

Penny didn't want to hurt the little girl's feelings, so she decided to try it. After all, if she didn't like it, she didn't have to eat it. She lifted a tiny bit on the tip of her spoon and tasted it cautiously. Then she laughed out loud, making heads turn in her direction.

"Chocolate pudding," she told a pair of men in three-piece suits at the next table. "I don't care what they call it, it tastes just like chocolate pudding and Cool Whip!"

Her bill came in a little leather binder, a miniature of the menu. She counted out fifteen dollars and fifty-seven cents, all in change, in orderly stacks on the table. She frowned, uncertain how much tip to leave. Roy never tipped more than 10 percent, but she'd seen the waitresses at Ponderosa sigh in disgust as she and Roy left the restaurant.

The waiter came over, staring at her as she counted out another ten dollars, all in quarters, setting them a discreet distance from the original coins.

"That's for the bill," she pointed as she stood up, "and that's for you, dear. It was a lovely meal. Thank you very much."

She felt giddy as she stepped out into the square, and wondered if the feeling was purely the effect of the Chablis. Except for a glass of champagne at Sandy's wedding the previous spring, Penny had never tasted alcohol. The champagne hadn't made her feel like this but had only given her a splitting headache. Then again, she thought, it may have been Roy's constant carping throughout the reception that made her head pound so fiercely. She'd actually snapped at him for the first time in her life.

"Oh, for mercy's sake, Roy Burford!" she had hissed at him. "She's our only daughter and this is the only wedding you'll ever have to pay for. You were the one who wanted prime rib, chicken kebobs, and shrimp on the buffet, and don't think I don't know why."

"And why is that?" he smirked. "You know so much, you tell me."

And she did. Everybody at Grace Baptist was still talking about how fine a spread Bill Colcamp had put out for his daughter Cindy's wedding last year. But Cindy's buffet hadn't had included any shrimp, and Roy just had to go Bill one better.

Roy had stalked off, his fists rammed in his

pockets, and didn't speak to her for the rest of the evening.

And that was just fine with Penny. If he thought his not speaking to her was any kind of hardship, then, boy howdy, did he have another think coming!

She took a walk around the square, admiring the begonias and impatiens. She hadn't felt this kind of easy happiness since—well, since delivering Christmas food and presents with her daddy.

By the time she got back into the Caddy, she knew exactly what she wanted to do with the hidden money.

chapter seven

The first thing Roy noticed when he opened the front door was the silence. No *Oprah* on the television, no sounds of chicken frying, not even the tick, tick, tick of the oven timer.

"Penny?"

He hoped the silence didn't mean she was on another one of her weird cooking binges. For a while, it had been chop suey and itty-bitty pancakes, all kinds of funny Chink food. He didn't know what got into her sometimes.

He sat his big orange thermos on the kitchen counter and tossed his cap on the back of a chair.

"Penny? Where the hell are you?"

He ambled through the den, pulling his keys

and stag-handled knife from his left pocket and dropping them onto the coffee table.

Damn it, he thought, moving toward the back of the house. Where in the hell was she?

That morning, she had complained of a headache as she washed the breakfast dishes. But she had kissed him goodbye—that little peck on the cheek—as he left for work, same as she did every morning.

He was already digging the loose change from the pocket of his overalls as he stepped into the bedroom.

"Penny? What are you doing in bed? You sick?"

Still no answer. She didn't stir at all.

Annoyance surged against Roy's skull, then fell back as another feeling, one completely alien and terrifying, crept into its place.

His fist opened. Two quarters, three dimes, and a single penny fell to the floor.

Small Change

❧ ❧ ❧

"Cerebral embolism," Dr. Clooney told Roy. "She went fast. Probably never even knew what hit her."

Dr. Clooney pushed his wire-rimmed glasses back on his nose as he explained about blood clots, arteries, and sudden ruptures. None of it made sense to Roy. He felt as though his insides had been scooped out and replaced with straw.

"How was she feeling this morning? Did she complain of dizziness, any tingling or numbness in her arms or legs?"

"She said she had a headache."

"Hmm. She must have gone back to bed after you left."

"She was only—only—" Hell, he couldn't remember how old his wife was! Had been. At that moment, he couldn't even remember his own age.

"Fifty-seven," Dr. Clooney supplied. "It's a shock, I know. But take comfort from the fact she didn't suffer. That's a mercy."

But his mind just wouldn't take it in. Not even when he called the kids. He said the words, but they were just sounds.

The house felt empty, too. The very walls seemed unsteady beneath his hands as he felt his way down the hall, as if brick and Sheetrock had turned to cardboard.

He couldn't bring himself to call anyone else. Not yet. The idea of telling it for the sixth time—he had already recounted it for the EMS operator, the paramedics, Dr. Clooney, Sandy and Carl—was more than he could bear. Instead he wandered the house, as if expecting Penny to suddenly pop from behind a door and tell him it had all been a mistake.

The next day, Sandy and Carl, both their spouses, and all five grandchildren crowded into the little house. But the place still felt as hollow as his own heart. Hollow and utterly dry.

Sandy asked her father if he had picked out a

dress to take to the funeral home yet. When he shook his head, she patted his shoulder.

"I'll take care of it, Daddy."

Roy didn't want to follow her into the bedroom and watch as she picked through Penny's Sunday dresses, but he wanted to hear all the obligatory phone calls even less. Listening to Carl's voice, repeating the same thing over and over, was even worse than facing Penny's clothes.

"She wasn't wearing any of her jewelry, was she?" Sandy asked as he hovered in the doorway. "I know she'd want to have her wedding ring and her gold cross, the one with the diamond chip—"

Roy said nothing. His daughter opened the jewelry box on the bureau, pushing the plated chains and plastic beads aside with one gentle finger. Then the expression on her face changed and she lifted an envelope from underneath the tangle of cheap jewelry.

She looked at the blank envelope for a full

minute, then looked at her father. When he offered no advice, she pulled a folded sheet of paper from the envelope.

"Oh, my God," she breathed, fresh tears welling her eyes. Her hand flew to her mouth. "Oh, my God."

"What?" her father asked.

"It's a letter. Dated 1978," Sandy sobbed, holding out the letter. "It's addressed to you, Daddy—"

Roy took the letter and read:

> *Dear Roy,*
>
> *If you're reading this, I must be dead. I hope it's years and years from now, but we just never know, do we? Dr. Clooney told me yesterday that the lump in my breast was just a cyst, but still, it got me thinking what would happen if I died before you. I know you're not good at this sort of thing, so I wanted to make it*

*as easy on you as I can. We've already
got the plots Daddy left us in Grace's
cemetery, so that's one less thing you'll
have to cope with. I want to be buried in
a white coffin with pink satin lining. I
know they make them like that, cause I
saw one on display at Sipple's when we
picked out your momma's casket. I know
it will probably cost a lot, but it's what I
want. It'll be real pretty, and I know
you'll like the way everybody will admire
it. Here is a check to help pay for it.*

A faded yellow check was paper-clipped
behind the letter. It was made out to cash in the
amount of $1,500.00.

"What the hell?" He stared at the amount,
written in his wife's careful schoolgirl script, and
then looked at the top left-hand corner.

He blinked. It wasn't even drawn on their
account at First American. Farmer's Union, it

said. And the name on the account was—was simply Penny Burford. What the hell—?

In the top of my closet, you'll find a box from Gaffer's. It's the dress I want to be buried in. Take it to the dry cleaner's first, though, to get the wrinkles out. Not Ralph's, though. Take it to Town and Country. Shirley at Ralph's will never get all those pleats to lay down right.

I want Brother Gary to do the sermon, and ask Betty Colcamp if she'll sing "Farther Along" and "Just As I Am." Maybe she can get Louise Milton to sing with her. They always did have such a nice harmony. I only hope, now that I'm dead, that Louise isn't still holding a grudge about me winning that bake-off for my red velvet cake. Tell her one last time, it weren't her recipe, it was my momma's.

About my headstone. Please don't put

my middle name on it; I always hated the name Mildred and I don't want that over my head for all eternity. Don't put Penelope, either. Just put Penny Harper Burford, the dates and then underneath: IT'S WHAT YOU DO WITH IT THAT COUNTS. Don't bother putting nothing like "Beloved Wife and Mother" on it. Everybody that matters will already know that part. Whenever I see that on somebody's headstone, I wonder who felt worse, the husband or the children. Surely they wouldn't put something like that on it unless they felt bad about something.

Last of all, Roy, tell Carl and Sandy that I love them, just as I love you. You've been a good husband, and I'm sorry I kept some things from you all these years. When you find out about them, and I know you will now that I'm gone, please don't think it means I didn't love you or

*trust you to provide for me and the kids.
You aren't your daddy, Roy. You are ten
times the man he was.*

> *Your loving wife,*
> *Penny*

*P. S. There are five silver dollars in
your daddy's ashtray. I want you to give
them to the kids. And for heaven's sake,
Roy, spend that change! You might be
surprised what you can do with it. For
that matter, spend that hundred-dollar bill
you been carrying around in your wallet.
Don't spend it on something just for other
people to admire, either. Spend it on
something that will make you happy.
Money isn't that important. It's what you
do with it that counts.*

Small Change

"I don't understand—" Roy looked down blankly at the top of his daughter's head. "Where'd this money come from?"

Sandy hardly heard her father's questions, uttered in a voice so soft and confused that it seemed to issue from a stranger's mouth. Instead, she was reading her mother's letter for herself, her lips moving slightly and tears running down her face.

Carl appeared in the doorway. Sarah and Paul crowded behind him.

"Momma, what's the matter?" Ten-year-old Sarah wiggled past her uncle and flew to Sandy.

Roy held out the check to his son, as if the faded slip of paper would answer all the questions in his face.

"Hell, you can't cash this," Carl said, frowning. "This check is more than twenty years old!"

"She's crying because Memaw's dead, stupid," eight-year-old Paul hissed. "Duh!"

"Shut up!" Sarah shouted, making Sandy wince.

"I don't have an account at no Farmer's Union." Roy's face flushed a dark, unhealthy purple. "They ain't even got a branch in Cairo—"

"Sarah! Paul! Both of you, hush!"

"It's from the one in Valdosta." Carl's voice strained to be heard over the din. He held the check up to the light, as if some magical clue might present itself. "It doesn't have your name on it, Dad. Just mom's. Must have been her account."

"Did you know she had an account of her own?" Sandy wiped her eyes with the back of the hand not clutching her sniffling daughter.

"No! How in the hell could she have a bank account?"

"Why would she go all the way to Valdosta to find a bank?" Carl asked.

"That's what I'm trying to tell ya!" Roy shouted. "She wouldn't have! Couldn't have! And she wouldn't have had nothing to put in it if she did!"

Small Change

Roy saw the look that passed from brother to sister. It was a fine thing when a man's children sat in judgment of him, he thought.

"Lookit, all I'm saying is she didn't need any bank account of her own," Roy grumbled, shoving his fists into his pockets and stalking out of the room. "I gave her whatever she needed. I took good care of your mother, and the both of you, too. You know damn well I did."

He didn't say much the rest of the afternoon, just sat in his Lazy Boy and stared at the television. He didn't seem to care what was on, or that the sound was muted.

"Just let him alone for a while," Cynthia, Carl's wife, told the kids. "Ya'll go and watch the TV in the back bedroom, okay?"

"Aw, Mom!" eleven-year-old Jason whined. "It's black and white. Nobody watches black and white TV anymore!"

"I wanna watch MTV," Scott chimed in.

Sandy found the Gaffer's box in the closet.

She thought her tears were under control until she shook out the purple dress. The slick polyester was beautiful, even if it was twenty years out of style.

"Aw, honey." Bobby, her husband, rubbed her back. "It's a nice dress. I can't imagine your momma in something that color, but it's really pretty."

"Oh, Bobby!" she sobbed.

She threw herself on the bed and cried for a solid hour. That beautiful dress, the tags still on it after twenty years hidden in the closet, was the saddest thing Sandy Burford Connelly had ever seen.

Every fifteen minutes or so, another person showed up on the stoop with a casserole, cake, or pie. Soon Corning and Tupperware hid every surface in the tiny yellow kitchen. The visitors just stood around the Formica table full of food, as if they'd come to pay homage to the feast, and talked in hushed voices.

Small Change

By the time Sandy could pull herself off the bedspread, her cheek had the imprint of chenille and Sarah was complaining that her stomach hurt.

"She ate all the chocolate pie!" Paul tattled. "Even after Aunt Cynthia told her not to hog it all!"

"Did not, you booger!" Sarah snapped back. "There's a whole half of it still left!"

Sandy padded into the den, wondering if she and Carl had been such horrors at eight and ten. And if Cynthia didn't wipe that damned smug expression off her face every time her kids hollered at each other. . . ."

"Hey, Daddy? You got any Pepto Bismal?"

"What's the matter? You sick?"

"No, it's Sarah. Just tell me where it is." Sandy was shocked to see her father getting to his feet. "I can find it."

"I can't tell you where it is," he said in a weary voice, "because I don't know exactly. I know your mother kept it in the bathroom some-where—"

He groaned as he bent over to peer under the sink, then groaned again as he straightened. She could hear his bones crack as he went to the narrow linen closet.

"What in the world are these still doing here?" Sandy reached around her father's bulk and picked up the box of Tampax. The box felt queer in her hands, heavier than it should have been. The contents shifted suddenly with an unexpected but strangley familiar sound. Sandy was about to open the box and peer inside, but her father's brusque voice distracted her.

"Hell, Sandy, you got two kids," Roy said, his color heating up. "You know more'n I do about that female hygiene stuff."

"But Momma went through the change ten years ago," Sandy muttered. Suddenly, she was furious with her father. "Didn't you notice?"

"Well, I guess not!" he shot back. "Apparently,

there was a hell of a lot about your momma I didn't notice! Like where she got fifteen hundred dollars! Take the damned things home with you, if you're so worried about it! I sure don't have any use for 'em!"

He shoved the pink bottle of Pepto Bismal at her so hard it knocked the Tampax box right out of her hands. The blue box fell to the floor and exploded in a shower of metal.

Sandy and her father both stood staring down at the coins that dotted the pink tile. A single quarter rolled round and round in ever-smaller circles near the toilet.

At the same moment, they both saw the registers.

"I just don't understand," Roy kept repeating. "It don't make sense."

"The first entry in this one is dated 1971," Carl said, flipping through the pages. "A deposit for $634.43—"

Carl looked up at his father.

"It just ain't possible!" Roy blurted. He ran his hand through his thinning, mostly gray hair.

"This one is 1976," Bobby offered, fanning the other register. "$2,023.97 is the first deposit—"

"Hey, is the date on that May 12?" Carl asked.

"Yep," Bobby nodded. "May 12."

"She withdrew the same amount from this account on the same day," Carl explained. "A withdrawal of $2,023.97 on May 12, leaving a balance of $156.21—"

Roy staggered to his feet.

"Daddy, where are you going?" Sandy cried.

"Valdosta!" he shot back, slamming the front door behind him.

Paul came careening up to his mother, crashing into her shoulder as he held out a shiny quarter for her inspection.

"Look what I found on Memaw and Papaw's bedroom floor!" he crowed. "Can I keep it?"

chapter eight

The man behind the desk looked up as the woman leaned near his ear, then looked over at Roy, silhouetted against the plate glass window. He stood up and walked to the large square rug beneath Roy's feet.

"David Tolson," the man said, extending his hand and smiling, but tensed as if steeled for the possibility of unpleasantness. "I'm the senior manager here. Mrs. Wofford said you wanted to talk to me about a confidential matter?"

This last was spoken with a lilt at the end, turning the statement into a question.

"Damn right I do." Roy felt less certain now that a hand was held out in front of him. He took it, squeezing the manager's soft, cool hand a bit harder than necessary. "I wanna find out about this here check."

He thrust the check under David Tolson's nose. The man leaned back, as if unable to focus, and took the slip of paper between two fingers.

"Yes, this is a check from one of our accounts," Tolson said. "A rather old check, if I may say so—"

"I can see that for myself," Roy snapped. "Is it still good?"

"Well—legally," David Tolson's voice drawled, full of long, lazy regret, "a check is considered invalid if not cashed within twelve months—"

"But is the money still here?"

David Tolson's face closed, the expression in his eyes turning flinty.

"I'm sorry, sir, I didn't catch your name—"

"Burford. Roy Burford. Penny Burford is my wife." Roy's voice caught, a sound like something torn deep inside his throat. "Was my wife. She died yesterday morning."

Tolson's eyes dipped to the check. When he looked up again at Roy's face, his features softened.

"Oh, I—I think I see. I'm sorry, Mr. Burford. I didn't realize. Your wife was a lovely woman. She hadn't been ill, had she?"

"You knew Penny? You knew my wife?"

David Tolson gingerly grasped Roy's elbow and led him to the desk at the very back of the room. The big man came along as meek as a child.

"Why, yes. Mrs. Burford was a longtime customer of this bank, and quite a favorite among the tellers in recent years. She was in here just last week—"

"You're telling me she did have an account here?" Roy's face went blank, and for a moment, David Tolson was afraid the man was going to keel over.

"Yes, sir." The manager lowered his voice and leaned forward. "I'm really not supposed to divulge this kind of information—client confidentiality, you understand. But under the circumstances, I don't think there's any harm in telling you that your wife had two accounts, actually. A checking account and a savings-investment fund account. You weren't aware of this?"

"No." All the bluster was gone from Roy's voice. He didn't know what he had expected—that the check was a fake? Some kind of joke? "I just found the check and the passbooks today."

"I don't understand though," David Tolson said thoughtfully, looking at the check still in his hands before handing it back to Roy. "Why would Mrs. Burford have left such a large check made out to cash lying around?"

"It was in a letter. A letter she left for me. She wanted me to use the check—" Roy swallowed. "To use the check to buy her a white casket with pink satin lining."

"I see." David Tolson pushed papers around on

his desk. "I'm so sorry for your loss, Mr. Burford. I know it sounds dreadfully impersonal, and this can certainly wait until a more appropriate time, but there are forms to be filled out, and we'll need a copy of the death certificate—"

"Why? What for?"

"Well—" David Tolson stared at him, his eyebrows rising. "To legally transfer the funds to you. Unless—did Mrs. Burford leave a will?"

"Hell," Roy sighed, wiping a hand across his eyes. His voice was thick with misery. "I don't know. I don't think so. Then again, I don't seem to know much of anything. After all this, I'm afraid to open a drawer in my own damned house. No telling what I'll find next. Are you married, Mr. Tolson?"

"Yes, I am."

"You think you know your wife pretty good, do you?"

"I should." David Tolson smiled. "Been married to the same woman for twenty-five years."

Roy's lips tightened as he smiled, and David Tolson thought he saw something like pity in the big man's bloodshot eyes.

"Penny and me were married for forty years. I never knew she had all this money hidden away. And I don't have no idea at all where it came from."

David Tolson guffawed, then brought a hand to his mouth guiltily as Roy glared.

"Please forgive me," he said somberly, the corners of his mouth straightening. "I don't mean to laugh. It's just—it's just that it's been something of a puzzle to us here at the bank, too."

When Roy said nothing, only continued to glare, David Tolson continued.

"Mrs. Burford is something of a legend here at Farmer's Union. She's the only customer to ever open a bank account with more than six hundred dollars all in change."

"Change?" Roy blinked.

"Change." David Tolson nodded. "Nickels,

Small Change

dimes, pennies——. You know. Small change."

"Small change," Roy parroted faintly.

"And all of her deposits—every single one, for almost thirty years—was the same. Always coins neatly rolled. For a while, the tellers had a pool every month to guess how much she was going to deposit on her next visit. The one who guessed closest won the pot."

"But change?" Roy's forehead furrowed and his eyes wrinkled, as if he had a massive headache. "Where did she get it?"

"Well, they guessed about that, too. Most of them were sure she must be a waitress or something—"

"My wife was no damned waitress! She never worked a day in her life! I provided for her and the kids just fine—"

"Hey, hey!" David Tolson raised his palms. "Please, Mr. Burford, I believe you! I didn't mean any disrespect. On the contrary. Your wife was very much admired around here. Heck, look up there over the window—"

Roy looked where David Tolson's finger
pointed. The granite over the tellers' windows
was carved in a deep inscription: A PENNY SAVED
IS A PENNY EARNED.

"People who believe in saving as much as your
wife did—" David Tolson wagged his head
gravely. "They are the reason we exist in the first
place. We thank our lucky stars for customers
like Mrs. Burford."

Roy settled back in the chair. His eyes still
glittered, but the rest of his face relaxed as if
slightly mollified.

"We don't have many customers who drive
in from out of town just to do their banking
with us, you understand. But Mrs. Burford
came in like clockwork, between one and two
o'clock on the first Monday of every month.
For the first five years, she only made deposits
and never took money out. I mean, never. Not
a cent."

Small Change

David Tolson leaned back in his chair, steepling his fingers in front of him.

"I had just started as a junior manager back then, a real eager beaver in those days! I was always looking for prospects for our savings and mutual fund programs, trying to impress my superiors with my enthusiasm, you understand. In fact, I was the one who approached Mrs. Burford about diverting some of her capital into a more profitable account, and investing the rest in mutual funds. And, as you can see in the registers you've found, she made quite a handsome turn around over the last twenty-nine years. Even when she finally started taking money out, it hardly made a dent in the principle—"

"What? She took money out? And you let her?"

"Well—yes, of course," David Tolson stammered, taken aback. "It was her money, Mr. Burford, after all."

"What in the hell did she do with it?"

"I have no idea, Mr. Burford. I'm sorry, but I just don't know."

Roy swore silently, then wiped his hand across his mouth.

"Well, can you tell me at least how much is left?"

"As I told you, there are legal issues to be—"

"I ain't asking you to give me any money," Roy Burford grunted. "I only wanna know how much money my wife left in her accounts. You can tell me that, cain't you?"

David Tolson got up and went over to a nearby desk where a woman sat typing into a computer. He whispered something to her, and she punched a series of buttons. Then David Tolson wrote something on a Post-it note and came back to Roy.

"That's it, Mr. Burford." He held out the yellow paper. "That's the total in both accounts as of today."

Small Change

Roy stared down at the figure printed neatly in blue ink.

Eleven thousand, four hundred and twenty-six dollars and seventeen cents.

chapter nine

"It was a lovely service," Betty Colcamp whispered, squeezing Roy's hands between her own. "Just lovely."

"Thank you so much," Sandy breathed as Betty's hand let go of Roy's and reached for hers. "For singing those songs Momma asked for. I never even heard that first one before, but I can see why she picked it."

"Oh, 'Farther Along' was always one of your momma's favorites." Betty blinked her wet eyes carefully, as if afraid her mascara would run. "Mine, too."

Bill shook Roy's hand stiffly.

"Such a sudden thing," he said, shaking his

head. "How you holding up?"

"All right, I guess." Roy's collar cut into his throat, but every time he tugged at it, Sandy shot daggers at him. As if Penny being dead meant he was supposed to be impervious to discomfort. It was ninety degrees with high humidity, and the sun beat down on his skull mercilessly.

"You come over and have dinner with us real soon." Betty patted his shoulder again, as if he were some old dog.

All these people, he thought. The church was never this full on an ordinary Sunday, except for maybe Easter and Christmas. He was sure he'd never even laid eyes on some of these people and wondered where they had come from.

He had expected Bill and Betty, of course, and Louise and Charles Miller. Penny's ancient Aunt Pauline, nearly ninety, wobbled around the cemetery, holding on to the arm of her oldest son, Beau, as she pointed out the straggly plots of Penny's parents and grandparents. The rest of

Small Change

Aunt Pauline's kids and grandkids trailed in her
wake as if she were royalty.

Even his brothers Tom and Buster had shown
up, looking hung-over as hell but wearing clean
shirts and clip-on ties. Tom's second wife,
Margie, was a scrawny bleached blonde whose
skin was tanned to leather. Margie kept pulling
her thin orange dress from the perspiration that
gathered in the cleft of her bosom, fanning herself with her flat little purse. Buster was on his
third wife—no, fourth—and Roy could not
remember her name for the life of him. She was
heavy in the hips, a good ten years younger than
Buster; her spike heels kept sinking into the
crumbling dirt so that every time she stood still,
she shrank an inch.

The little old ladies from church were no surprise, either. They came to every funeral, as if it
were another Sunday meeting that they didn't
dare miss or risk hellfire and damnation. He rec-
ognized Miss Lucille, Miss Clarice, and hump-

backed little Nadine Turner. Luther White and Arnell Turnbull were there, too, looking like a couple of old crows in black suits that smelled faintly of mothballs and Aqua-Velva.

What did surprise him was the handful of teenagers lingering awkwardly at the back of the church. They didn't seem connected to any of the adults; one of them even had a stud in her nose, so he didn't think they belonged to anybody he or Penny knew. They clumped together even as everyone moved out to the graveside.

"Mr. Burford?" the girl with the nose stud approached him haltingly, glancing over her shoulder at the others that hung back. She had apparently been appointed their spokesman. "We just wanted to tell you we're really sorry about your wife. She was always so nice whenever she came in."

"Uh, thank you." Roy couldn't seem to stop staring at the gold button poking through the girl's left nostril. He knew he'd sound foolish, but he had to ask. "When she came in where?"

"Oh, the Burger King over on Aberdeen," the girl said, hiding a nervous twitch of her lips behind her hand. She twisted about on one foot. "We all, like, you know, work there."

"The Burger King?" Carl leaned over his daddy's shoulder.

"Uh-huh."

"Do you—do you always go to your customer's funerals?" The flash of gold mesmerized Roy. Burger King, he thought. Burger King?

"Oh, no!" The girl's hand flew to her mouth again. "That would be creepy. But Penny—"

"Penny?" Roy repeated.

"She told me to call her that. But I guess I should say Mrs. Burford now—she was real nice. She came in every week just about." The girl gave him a smile so sweet that Roy almost forgot the nose stud. "Most people, you know, they just want their food and correct change and, bam, they're outta there! But Penny—Mrs. Burford—

she would always ask us how we were doing, and how we liked our jobs and stuff—"

"Sometimes she'd sit and talk to us on our breaks," a lanky boy with a mop of frizzy hair interjected. "When Judy's boyfriend dumped her that time—"

He jerked his thumb at a dumpy blond girl behind him. Her heavy mascara was smudged down one cheek as if she'd been crying, but she gave Roy a sparkly-eyed, shy smile when he looked at her.

"And she couldn't do nothing but cry for a solid week, and the manager said he'd fire her if she didn't stop crying in front of the customers—"

"Yeah," the nose-stud girl nodded enthusiastically. "That's when she told Mr. Petrie to leave Judy be and then she sat and talked to Judy for a solid hour—"

"She was really cool," the frizzy-haired boy nodded sagely. "Your wife, I mean. Not Judy. She's kind of a dork."

Small Change

Roy stared at the teenagers as they ambled away.

"Well, that was strange," Carl whispered. "Did you know—"

"Hell, no!" Roy snapped.

"Daddy!" Sandy hissed.

He had nodded at the polite condolences as everyone filed past his seat on their way to peer down into the gleaming white casket. Then he had listened to Brother Gary's eulogy while staring straight ahead at the shiny line of pink satin visible from where he sat. He wondered what they'd all say if he told them what he was really thinking.

He was thinking about the money, mostly. Where had it come from? Eleven thousand, four hundred and twenty-six dollars and seventeen cents. And what had Penny done with the money she'd taken out?

When he'd got home from Valdosta and his talk with David Tolson, Roy had gone through the two bank registers with a calculator, pad, and pencil. There was only one withdrawal each year, always on the first Monday of December. In 1976, Penny had taken out $500 in cash. The following two years, she withdrew $700. In 1979, the amount was $850.

"It looks like she never took out more than the accrued interest," Bobby had ventured. Bobby was an accountant who understood such things. He had explained to Roy how even as little as twenty dollars, wisely invested, would mushroom over nearly thirty years.

After the casket was lowered into the ground, Sandy slipped beside her father and leaned into him.

"I just had the weirdest conversation with Mr. Toomey," she said.

"Who?"

"Mr. Toomey. You know, the old guy who still runs the Rialto downtown?"

"I thought they closed it down," Roy muttered. He knew who Mr. Toomey was, everybody did; but Roy didn't think he'd ever actually spoken to the man. Roy hadn't gone to the picture show since he and Penny were dating. He saw no point in paying money to sit with a bunch of strangers, in a room that smelled of stale popcorn, when he could stay home and watch television for free. "What the hell is Toomey doing here?"

"Well, I sort of asked him the same thing," Sandy said. "I mean, I didn't think you and Momma ever went to the movies, and Mr. Toomey isn't even a member of Grace. But he told me that Momma did go to the movies. A lot."

Roy stared at her.

"He said she always went to the afternoon matinees," Sandy continued. "Sometimes two and three times a week, if they were showing something she liked. He said she sat through *An Officer and a Gentleman* six times in two weeks, and came three days in a row when they re-released *Gone with the Wind* a couple of years back. Did you know—"

"No! Damn it, I didn't know! Are you telling me your mother spent $17,400 on movies and Burger King?"

"Daddy, would you please lower your voice," Sandy hissed. "Let me finish what I started telling you, please? Mr. Toomey said he used to have coffee with Momma sometimes between the matinee and the evening shows. They would talk about the movies and—Daddy, don't look like that. You know it wasn't anything like that! Goodness, Mr. Toomey is old enough to be Momma's daddy!"

Sandy thought her mother must have befriended Mr. Toomey out of pity. That would be just like her momma. Mr. Toomey was nearly eighty years old. His wife had died in a car wreck years and years ago, and his only son had died in Vietnam. The Rialto was all Mr. Toomey had left.

Her father glared at her, and Sandy decided

she wouldn't tell him the rest. Not about the books she'd found in the bottom of her old bedroom closet, or the three-ring binders crammed with notes. At first, Sandy thought they were some of her old schoolbooks, but then she found a handful of grade slips from Valdosta State. The name on the slips was Penny Burford.

Her momma had made an A in English Romantic Poets in 1981 and a B- in Modern Literature in 1983. She earned another A, this time in Introduction to Pottery, in 1984. Apparently, Penny had had some trouble with Botany 101 in 1985, getting a C-. In 1986, she had taken Life Drawing and A Survey of Renaissance Art, earning a B and an A respectively. Pushed far in the back of the closet, Sandy had found her mother's sketch pad, filled with charcoal drawings of naked women. She couldn't say whether they were any good or not; she was too surprised that her mother had even tried it in the first place.

It seemed that her mother had taken whatever classes struck her fancy, with no thought to earning an actual degree. Despite a preponderance of art and literature courses, Penny had also taken classes in horticulture, basic accounting, small appliance repair, and Chinese cooking.

No, Sandy decided. She would not tell her father about any of that. If he couldn't handle his mother going to the movies, then the very idea of Penny going to college might give him a stroke. She wished her mother had told her about all this, though. But Sandy supposed it was enough to have found out about it now. Discovering her mother's secret life took away some of the sadness she'd felt ever since pulling that purple dress out of the Gaffer's box.

Her momma had had more of a life than Sandy ever imagined.

Thank God, she thought, blinking away tears. Thank God.

chapter ten

As car doors slammed in the blacktop parking lot, Brother Gary Foster walked over to Roy Burford.

Roy stood alone, watching the two men pat their spades over the lumpy earth of his wife's grave.

"I just had a talk with Sandy and Carl," Brother Gary said. "You've got two fine children, Roy. You and Penny did a good job with them."

"They tell you to come over here and try to talk to me?" Roy squinted at the pastor in the slanting sun. "I told 'em to go on back home."

"Oh, they went, they went. Said they'd see you at the house in a little while."

Brother Gary and Roy stood watching the men reposition the green squares of sod in companionable silence.

Gary Foster was used to Roy Burford's silences. When he took over the church from Penny's father, he had paid special attention to his predecessor's daughter and widow, concentrating more on Penny and her family after her mother passed away. He knew that preachers' families put up with a lot. A preacher was called, but his family just got swept along whether they liked it or not. And yet he knew that it was hard for them to see a stranger standing in the pulpit that had been the center of their universe for so long.

He had never really warmed to Roy, but he'd grown to like Penny Burford very much. She was his favorite kind of Christian, and, he thought, the rarest. A believer who actually listened to his sermons. Who came to church, not to show off a new dress, but to refill her spirit from God's well. He could see it in her face every Sunday, the way her polite, tense smile relaxed and spread into an easy visible grace by the time the final chord of the last hymn died away.

She was a Christian who never got caught up in the petty squabbles and politics that sprouted wherever more than three human beings gathered. Who never spouted Bible verses to exalt or excuse herself, or to judge others. A quiet, gentle woman with a bottomless heart, who lived like a real Christian instead of just acting like one.

He'd known these things about Penny Burford even before she befriended his wife. Poor Wendy, who often had a hard time sharing her husband with a congregation of two hundred needy souls. Wendy, who had died of cancer four years ago. Penny Burford could have been an unrepentant adulterer, closet alcoholic or kleptomaniac, and Gary Foster would have forgiven her of all those faults, just for the kindness she had shown Wendy, both before and after her illness was diagnosed. Wendy had needed a friend very badly, and Penny had taken up the burden graciously. Only a preacher's daughter could know just how much a preacher's wife needed one friend in whom she could confide with impunity.

Roy Burford, however, was another matter. Gary Foster knew that Roy's weekly attendance was merely a social habit; like many of his congregation, Roy Burford came to church because that was what a respectable man did. He mouthed the hymns, tugged at his tie, yawned during the sermon, put a dollar in the offering plate and then went home to watch football.

Still, Gary's heart went out to Roy now. The man had shuffled through his wife's funeral with a scowl of vague incomprehension, and frequently looked around as if he wasn't quite sure where he was or why he was there. Gary understood what it was to keep looking around for the other half of your life, only to remember it was gone and never coming back.

"Well, Sandy did say something to me about

speaking with you," Brother Gary finally confessed. He kept staring straight ahead, not wanting to crowd Roy with too direct a gaze. "She's just naturally worried about you. Her mother's death coming so sudden like it did. I told her you were a strong man. That'd you'd work through your grief in your own time."

That wasn't all he'd told Sandy, of course. Sandy was upset that her father hadn't shed a tear—at least that she'd seen—and that he wasn't talking to anybody.

"Give him time," Brother Gary had told her. "A man like your father doesn't like to show his own hurt, least of all to his children. Everybody copes with grief in their own way."

"I can't go back to the house just yet." Roy's voice was low and raspy. "I just don't understand any of this."

Gary Foster opened his mouth, about to murmur the programmed responses of a hundred funerals or more. How death was a natural part of life, how the deceased had gone on to a heavenly reward and how we would all be reunited in Christ one day. But he stopped himself. If he didn't find any comfort in those words today, then neither would Roy Burford.

Somehow Gary Foster got the impression that it wasn't just the reality of his wife's death that confounded Roy right now anyway. The man seemed angry, in a lost and dazed sort of way, as if he couldn't figure out just who he was mad at.

"You don't need me to tell you Penny was a special woman," Brother Gary said. "I'm sure you know that."

Roy didn't say anything for a moment.

"A lot of people came for the funeral," he sighed finally. He spoke stiffly, like a man trying to make small talk at a cocktail party. "Penny would have been pleased, I guess—"

"She will be missed around here, that's for sure."

Brother Gary rocked back on his heels. He

Small Change

and Roy watched the two men from Sipple's Mortuary rearrange the flowers in front of the bright new headstone, then dust their hands on their khakis and walk toward their truck.

"It's what you do with it that counts," Brother Gary read from the headstone, his smile breaking wide. "Truer words were never spoken. Or carved, as the case may be."

"I don't have no idea what it means," Roy said. "But that's what she wanted, so that's what I told 'em to put."

Brother Gary turned and looked at Roy directly for the first time. Roy must have seen the surprise in his expression, for the big man glared hotly at him.

"You know what she meant by that?" Roy shoved his hands deeper into his pockets. "'Cause if you do, I'd like you to explain it to me. I wish to hell somebody could explain a lot of stuff to me."

Brother Gary hesitated.

"Well—. I think it was sort of a motto for her, you know? She must have said that to me a hundred times over the years." Brother Gary chuckled, a low laugh of self-deprecation as he shook his head. "Especially when she wanted to get me into that Santa costume."

Roy stared at him.

"I know, it was for the kids and I shouldn't have felt so foolish." Brother Gary grinned. "But dressing up like that bothered me in the beginning. I mean, I'm supposed to be a man of God, all dignified and solemn—"

"What the hell are you talking about?" Roy's bottom lip hung limply, turning his mouth into a dark, down-turned crescent.

Now it was Brother Gary's turn to stare.

"Why, the Santa project, of course." His pale blue eyes opened and shut. "Every Christmas—. She always swore me to secrecy. But I thought surely you knew about it."

Roy said nothing, only gazed down at his

shoes with humiliation creeping into his cheeks.

"Oh, my," the pastor breathed softly, his eyes widening with amazement. "You didn't know about the Santa project?"

"Brother Gary, there's a lot I didn't know about." Roy met his eyes, but his voice held a note of defeat. "The day after Penny died, I found out she'd had a bank account of her very own. She never said nothing to me about it. Then I find out, not only did she have this bank account she kept secret, but she had a shit-load of money—"

Roy swallowed, wiping a hand over his glistening forehead.

"I'm sorry, Brother Gary. But she had a lot of money in that account. I don't know where it came from, or what she spent it on—"

The big man's voice broke.

"It's all right, Roy." The pastor laid a hand on his shoulder. "Anything you tell me is in confidence. I'm your minister, remember? I wouldn't be here if I didn't know how to keep my mouth shut."

"I don't understand. Sandy's mad at me 'cause she thinks I just care about the money. I don't give a damn about the money. Not now. But I never thought Penny kept secrets from me. We were married for forty years! And now I find out she's got more than eleven thousand dollars in the Farmer's Union in Valdosta. Where in the hell does a woman like my wife get that kind of money? That's not even counting the seventeen-thousand it looks like she spent over the last twenty years—"

"I thought you knew," Brother Gary murmured. "I swear, I thought you knew."

"Well, I didn't!" Tears ran down Roy's cheeks. He fumbled in his suit pocket for the white hankie and honked his nose.

"Roy, I swear to you, I know one thing for certain. Penny never meant to hurt you. That's the last thing she intended to happen."

"How do you know that?" Roy's smirk was further twisted by the grimace of his silent tears. "Do you know where the money came from? Or what she spent it on?"

"The money came from you, Roy. And in a way, I think she spent it trying to make up for hurt she thought she caused somebody a long time ago."

"Huh? From me? No, that's not possible. Did she tell you that? 'Cause it ain't true—"

"Roy Burford, for once in your life would you just shut up and listen?"

Roy straightened. His eyes narrowed.

"All right," he growled. "I'm listening."

"Penny came to me one day with a problem. She said it had been weighing on her mind for a long time."

"Uh-huh."

"She said you always left a lot of small change laying around the house. She said it used to drive her crazy, all that money that you wouldn't ever spend. So she started taking it and putting it in the bank. And after awhile, there was too much of it to give back without your noticing."

"Change?" Roy's voice was weak with wonder. "My change? That cain't be."

"Hell, think about it Roy. A man empties the change out of his pockets every day of his life for thirty years, it's bound to build up. And you obviously never missed it."

"But—but why didn't she tell me?"

"I don't know, but I can guess."

Brother Gary frowned. He couldn't very well say: Because you're a horse's ass, Roy Burford, and how Penny managed to love you, I'll never know. Oh, Lord, how many marriages just like the Burford's had he seen over the years? Marriages of competent, intelligent women who spent their lives tiptoeing around a husband's prickly pride? He chose his words carefully.

"Because Penny was trying to be a good and obedient wife. She was afraid you'd be angry, and she was right. But she couldn't stand to see that money just sitting there. You didn't seem to want it. You wouldn't spend it. So she did something with that little bit of change you threw away every day. Because it's what you do with it that counts."

☙ ☙ ☙

Roy listened to Brother Gary's voice with fierce concentration. He listened, but he couldn't seem to stop reading those deep lines carved in Penny's headstone.

It's what you do with it that counts.

He thought about Penny's letter, and now it began to make sense.

I'm sorry I kept some things from you all these years. When you find out about them—please don't think it means I didn't love you or trust you to provide for me and the kids. You aren't your daddy, Roy. You are ten times the man he was.

She had been talking about the money, of course. That was why she'd left that check. She had known it couldn't be cashed, but that it would lead him to the rest of it. One way or another, it would pay for the white casket with the pink satin lining.

With painful clarity, he saw that Penny had known him better than he knew himself. *You aren't your daddy, Roy.*

Somehow, she had known his secrets. She had understood that he'd made a silent promise the day he proposed to her. A promise that she would never have to go down to the county extension office and beg for food stamps the way his momma had. That he would never set foot in a bar or a liquor store, that he'd never waste money on Jim Beam, whores, cigars, and poker games like his daddy did.

"Penny came to me sometime in 1976," Brother Gary was saying.

"I remember 'cause it was the Bicentennial. She had some money that she wanted to use for the church's Christmas ministry. And I was only too pleased to accept it. With the recession, the Christmas baskets were getting so skimpy that I was almost embarrassed to pass 'em out. Then the church had to have a new roof, and then the boiler had to be replaced. One thing after another, you know how it is. A church is no different from an ordinary family, Roy. There's never enough money for everything that needs to get done."

Roy felt a sudden anger bubbling up inside him. His throat burned with it as the hands in his pockets clenched into fists. Charity, damn it to hell! Penny had spent all that money on charity! She was still the preacher's daughter, doing her good deeds no matter how much she humiliated other people! Oh, she didn't know what it was like to have strangers standing on your front porch, looking down their noses at you, thinking they were better than you because they gave you their second-hand clothes—

Oh, she might have forgotten that day on his

front porch, but he sure as hell hadn't! The preacher's daughter with that big red bow in her hair and a new winter coat, staring at him with those big brown eyes—

Hadn't she understood how much that had hurt him? Damn her!

"Only she had one little string attached to her offer." Brother Gary smiled. "I had to dress up in a Santa Claus suit when I delivered the packages."

The roaring in Roy's ears suddenly stilled. The silence stunned him.

"She had this funny idea that made a lot of sense when she explained it to me," Brother Gary continued. "All these years as a minister, I'd thought that the people I helped understood I was only the messenger. A stand-in for Christ, so to speak."

The pastor's words burned into his brain, as if he'd never really heard anything before in his whole life. Roy's chest ached with shame.

"But I never put myself in their shoes, you see.

Small Change

I never stopped to think that some people—even the kids—might think I was—I don't know. Rubbing their noses in their situation, I guess. That's what made Penny such an extraordinary woman, Roy. She thought about things like that. She didn't just want to help people, she wanted to do it in a way that let them keep their pride.

"She talked me into not using the food baskets at all," Brother Gary continued. "She remembered when she helped her own father deliver the baskets, how the cans were usually dented and the labels peeling. You know, lots of people mean well, but they just use the food drive as an excuse to clean out their pantries. We'd get six dozen cans of lima beans, half of them past their expiration date—"

Or, Roy thought, swallowing a hard knot in his throat, you got things like asparagus. Funny brands of things your own momma never bought, when she had the money for groceries.

Oh, God—.

"Penny's idea was to use gift certificates. We mailed them anonymously. Then they could go to the Piggly Wiggly and get whatever they needed. What they wanted to eat for Christmas dinner, not whatever other people didn't want.

"But for kids, we still delivered toys and clothes. Not used, though. Penny said that no kid wanted to play in their front yard wearing clothes somebody else might recognize as their hand-me-downs—"

Roy had a memory of his mother, buttoning him into a second-hand coat, swearing that nobody would know it came from the church donation box. But they had. Cruel little bastards, children. They always knew. And they always teased.

I know your drunk daddy didn't buy that coat, he could hear Martin Baker hooting, *'cause it's mine!*

And then they had held him down on the

playground, smashing his face in the dirt, until Martin yanked the coat down around his shoulders and exposed the name tag still sewn there. Martin Baker, it said.

"She organized yard sales for the donated stuff. People who didn't have a lot of money could come and pick things out for themselves, right along side of those who could afford better but just wanted to help out the church. All those women could look each other in the eye and say they all had to do their part to help a good cause. No shame on anybody's part.

"She was a whiz at organizing those things. Then we took the money we raised and added Penny's money to it and went shopping for new stuff. She even talked some of the stores into giving us discounts, since it was for charity."

Roy remembered Penny talking about the church rummage sales, but she never mentioned that she was the one in charge. Never mentioned what she was raising money for. And he knew, now, why she hadn't told him. She was sparing him the hurt of remembering things he'd tried all his life to forget.

"Penny never called it charity, of course. She said charity might have been the greatest of gifts in Christ's time, but that most people today equated charity with a handout. Charity was something given that wasn't deserved or earned. No, she always called it a good cause. Or simply helping out. 'Everybody deserves to be helped out from time to time,' she used to say."

Oh, Penny, he thought. Oh, Penny.

How she had loved Christmas. She'd always been happiest during the holidays. Especially the last few years. Now he understood that sparkle in her eyes, the rosy glow of her cheeks that always peaked at the end of December. He had thought it was just the cold weather and too many sugar cookies. But it had been more than that.

"She was a tiger about that Santa costume," Brother Gary laughed. "She insisted I had to look like the genuine article. I told her that the older kids would know there was no Santa, that I was just somebody in a red suit and beard. But she said that wasn't the point. The point, according to Penny, was that Santa Claus visited everybody, rich and poor alike. And I don't think more than a handful of people ever figured out who we were—"

"We?"

Brother Gary laughed again.

"Oh, yes. Penny went with me. She insisted on it." The pastor's blue eyes twinkled. "She dressed like Mrs. Claus. Gray wig, little wire-rimmed spectacles, the works. She made a real pretty Mrs. Claus."

Roy, to his own astonishment, began to laugh. It started with a small smile that traveled up into his cheeks, making the flesh curve into his eyes. He was picturing Penny in a bright red dress, trimmed with lace perhaps, or one of those frilly old-fashioned aprons. In his mind's eye, the wig was brilliant white, a mass of curls, and the little glasses kept sliding down her pug nose. She had always had the cutest nose.

The laugh swelled in his belly, then whooped from his throat. He laughed until he had to bend over with his hands on his knees, tears streaming down his face.

And when the laughter died, he was sobbing.

He couldn't stop. He didn't know how long he stood there in the empty cemetery, just him and Brother Gary. The preacher patted his back a couple of times, but said nothing.

He was embarrassed when he finally caught his breath and wiped his eyes. But when he looked at Brother Gary, he saw the preacher's cheeks were wet, too.

"I know, Roy. Believe me, I know. I sometimes think we men are the dullest of God's creatures. We never know just what we've got until it's gone."

The two widowers walked in silence toward

the parking lot. Roy's Cadillac and Brother Gary's dark blue Taurus were the only cars there.

"You gonna keep doing the Santa thing?" Roy asked in a strained voice.

"I'm gonna try." Brother Gary smiled. "It gets to be an addiction of sorts. Helping others."

Roy nodded.

"Could you use a hand, do you think?" He did not look at the preacher, but studied his key ring carefully to find the right one, as if he didn't know it purely by touch. "Or at least, some money?"

"Oh, we can always use that."

"I think I got some lying around."

Brother Gary grinned through his open window as he started the engine.

"Good one, Roy."

Roy walked over to Brother Gary's car and drew out his wallet. His fingers closed around the hundred-dollar bill and pulled it out.

"Consider this your first donation," he said,

handing him the bill. "I don't need it anymore."

Brother Gary nodded.

"See you on Sunday, Roy."

"Yep. See ya Sunday."

He watched the Taurus crunch out of the lot, then turned toward his own car. He had better get on home before the kids sent out a search party. There would be a house full of people, but he thought he could stand it now.

The descending sun shone across the windshield and flashed on something bright near his left foot. For a moment, he wondered if the little girl from Burger King had lost her nose stud.

He bent down and picked it up.

A penny. A bright, new penny.

Roy Burford slipped it into his pocket and got in the car.

The End

"It's what you do with it that counts."